The Little Bear Loves Her Gammy

The Little Bear loves the way
her Gammy cooks.

The Little Bear loves
the way her Gammy
keeps her clean.

The Little Bear loves
the way her Gammy hugs.

The Little Bear loves
the way her Gammy plays.

The Little Bear loves
the way her Gammy teaches.

The Little Bear loves
the way her Gammy dances.

The Little Bear loves
the way her Gammy
grows flowers.

The Little Bear loves her Gammy
because she is beautiful
inside and out.

The Little Bear loves
the way her Gammy
keeps her safe.

The Little Bear loves
the way her Gammy
takes care of her
when she is sick.

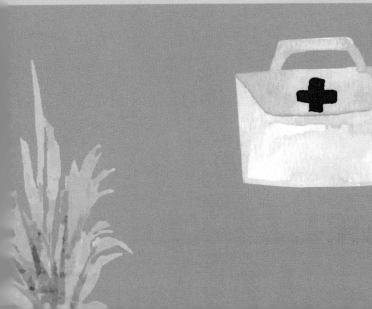

The Little Bear loves
the way her Gammy
reads her bedtime stories.

The Little Bear loves the way her Gammy kisses her goodnight.

Made in the USA
Las Vegas, NV
16 December 2023

83008089R00017